D0580131

• M. SATIE ET SON AMI, FORTIE,
SUR LES CHAMPS-ELYSÉES AVEC
LA TOUR EIFFEL. •

Paris

CARTE POSTALE

My dear Niece and Nephew,

My traveling companion,
Ffortusque, and I
will be arriving from PARIS
very soon to spend the
summer with all of you.
What adventures we have
to tell you about!
love,
your Uncle Satie *

Rosalie + Conrad Abbey
110 Main St.
Centerville, MIDWEST
U.S.A.

• PAR AVION •

* Pronounced sah-*tee*.

PARIS

CENTERVILLE

Tomie dePaola

MR. SATIE AND THE GREAT ART CONTEST

Originally published as *Bonjour, Mr. Satie*

PUFFIN BOOKS

For Joy, who named *Fortie*;
Gene, who introduced me to *Gertrude* and *Alice*
and made me name *Satie*;
Luis, who helped with photos of the Paris crowd
and who always makes me giggle;
and Joe, who never knew *Satie*
but loves *Dayton*.

PUFFIN BOOKS
Published by the Penguin Group
Penguin Young Readers Group, 345 Hudson Street, New York, New York 10014, U.S.A.
Penguin Group (Canada), 90 Eglinton Avenue East, Suite 700, Toronto, Ontario,
Canada M4P 2Y3 (a division of Pearson Penguin Canada Inc.)
Penguin Books Ltd, 80 Strand, London WC2R 0RL, England
Penguin Ireland, 25 St Stephen's Green, Dublin 2, Ireland
(a division of Penguin Books Ltd)
Penguin Group (Australia), 250 Camberwell Road, Camberwell, Victoria 3124, Australia
(a division of Pearson Australia Group Pty Ltd)
Penguin Books India Pvt Ltd, 11 Community Centre, Panchsheel Park,
New Delhi - 110 017, India
Penguin Group (NZ), Cnr Airborne and Rosedale Roads, Albany, Auckland 1310,
New Zealand (a division of Pearson New Zealand Ltd)
Penguin Books (South Africa) (Pty) Ltd, 24 Sturdee Avenue, Rosebank,
Johannesburg 2196, South Africa

Registered Offices: Penguin Books Ltd, 80 Strand, London WC2R 0RL, England

First published in the United States of America by G. P. Putnam's Sons,
a division of Penguin Putnam Books for Young Readers, 1991
Published by Puffin Books, a division of Penguin Young Readers Group, 2007

10 9 8 7 6 5 4 3 2 1

THE LIBRARY OF CONGRESS HAS CATALOGED THE G. P. PUNTAM'S SONS EDITION AS FOLLOWS:
dePaola, Tomie.
Bonjour, Mr. Satie / written and illustrated by Tomie dePaola
p. cm.
Summary: Through the diplomatic efforts of Uncle Satie, two talented Parisian artists end their feud.
ISBN: 0-399-21782-7 (hc)
[1. Artists—Fiction. 2. Uncles—Fiction. 3. Paris (France)—Fiction.]
I. Title. II. Title: Mister Satie, Paris.
PZ7.D439Mr 1991 [E]—dc20 90-37633 CIP AC
Typography by Nanette Stevenson.

Puffin Books ISBN 978-0-14-240771-4

Manufactured in China

Ever since the postcard arrived from Paris, Rosalie and Conrad had been waiting for the arrival of their uncle —Mr. Satie, world traveler—and his companion, Ffortusque Ffollet, Esq. Every day they asked Mama and Papa when they would arrive.

"Hello, hello, Uncle Satie," cried Rosalie and Conrad. "Hello, hello, Mr. Ffortusque Ffollet."

"Hello, hello, everyone," cried the visitors. And they all hugged and kissed and went inside.

"Now that we're here, my dears," Mr. Satie said, "Fortie is going to cook us a fabulous French dinner."

"A special recipe from Alice and Gertrude, our dear American friends living in Paris," said Fortie. And off he went to the kitchen.

"What adventures did you have this trip, Uncle Satie?" Rosalie and Conrad asked.

"Well, *mes enfants,* do you remember my friend Pablo, who painted that portrait of me in blue? Well, his new paintings are very different. They caused quite a stir in Paris this spring."

"Oh, tell us, tell us!" cried the children.

"Well, it all began the Sunday we arrived in Paris. Fortie and I were sitting in our favorite café, when who should come along but..."

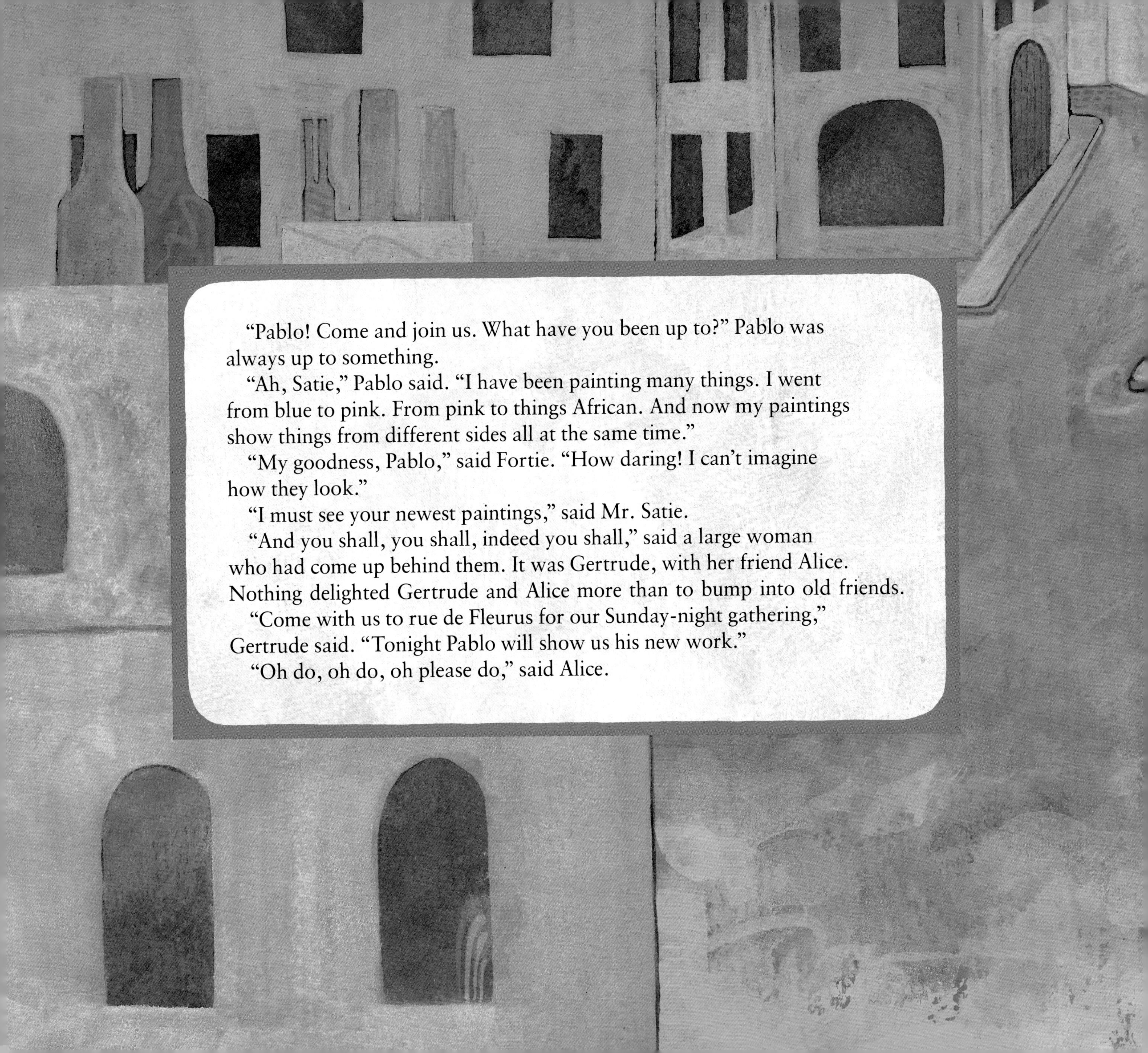

"Pablo! Come and join us. What have you been up to?" Pablo was always up to something.

"Ah, Satie," Pablo said. "I have been painting many things. I went from blue to pink. From pink to things African. And now my paintings show things from different sides all at the same time."

"My goodness, Pablo," said Fortie. "How daring! I can't imagine how they look."

"I must see your newest paintings," said Mr. Satie.

"And you shall, you shall, indeed you shall," said a large woman who had come up behind them. It was Gertrude, with her friend Alice. Nothing delighted Gertrude and Alice more than to bump into old friends.

"Come with us to rue de Fleurus for our Sunday-night gathering," Gertrude said. "Tonight Pablo will show us his new work."

"Oh do, oh do, oh please do," said Alice.

PAIN · BRIOCHE · PAIN

All of Paris was interested in art. Gertrude's Salon (for that is what the Sunday-night gathering was called) was *the* place where *the* interesting people came to discuss interesting things. Everyone was glad to see Mr. Satie. "Bonjour, Mr. Satie!" The Salon was already filled with people. How they talked. How they laughed. How they argued.

Suddenly everyone was quiet. Henri had come in. Henri was a painter too. He looked a little like a bank clerk.

"Henri, Henri, Henri," said Gertrude. "You are back from Nice so soon. [Nice is in the south of France.] Was Nice nice?"

"Yes, Gertrude," Henri said. "Nice was nice, and I did some nice paintings in Nice. I have brought them to show you."

Pablo glowered.

"Oh dear, Satie," Fortie whispered. "I smell trouble."

"But I'm showing *my* new paintings tonight," said Pablo. "Gertrude said I could."

Pablo put his paintings against one wall.
Henri put his paintings against the other.
Everyone started talking at once, taking sides.
"Pablo is brilliant! Henri is boring!" shouted one group.
"Henri is a genius! Pablo is weird!" shouted the other group.

"Oh, oh, oh," cried Alice.
"A duel!" the Russian prince shouted.
"A prizefight!" yelled the American writer.
"Call the gendarme!" screamed Pablo's wife.
"Enough, enough, enough," bellowed Gertrude.
And they all stopped at once.

"We shall have a contest," Gertrude announced. "Pablo and Henri will hang their paintings in Monsieur V's gallery, and someone will judge them."

"But who will be the judge?" asked the lady poet from England.

"Well," Ffortusque Ffollet spoke up. "There is one among us who not only knows all about paintings but is fair and honest and true. And that is my dear friend, Mr. Satie."

"Yes, yes, yes," said Gertrude, and everyone agreed.

All of Paris buzzed.

All of Paris was interested.

All of Paris held its breath.

The day of the judging arrived. Gertrude and Alice, Pablo and Henri, and Fortie accompanied Mr. Satie to the gallery. A huge crowd followed. Reporters from all the newspapers were there. Monsieur V greeted the crowd and led Mr. Satie inside.

GALLERIE V

PABLO
PABLO
PABLO
PABLO
PABLO
LE JOURNA

Finally, Mr. Satie appeared at the door.

"Well, Satie?" Gertrude asked.

"After careful consideration," said Mr. Satie, "I have concluded that to compare Henri's paintings of Nice with Pablo's paintings of newspapers, guitars, and faces from all different sides would be to compare apples with oranges. Both are delicious but *taste* totally different.

"Pablo's and Henri's paintings are also both delicious but *look* totally different. I declare the contest a—draw!"

The crowd cheered.

"Vive Pablo! Vive Henri! Vive Mr. Satie!"

33311

Gertrude and Alice gave Mr. Satie big kisses because he had saved the day. After all, they loved both Henri and Pablo. Pablo and Henri shook hands with each other and then with Mr. Satie.

The crowd cheered and lifted Henri, Pablo, and Mr. Satie onto their shoulders and marched down the boulevard to the café, where they had a party.

“So you can see that art is alive and well in Paris,” said Mr. Satie. Rosalie and Conrad clapped their hands.

“Dinner’s ready!” announced Fortie, and they all went in to the dining room and sat down to a delicious meal.

"And now for some presents," said Mr. Satie.
"Paint sets!" shouted Conrad.
"From Paris!" cried Rosalie.
"And tomorrow we will go out and paint together," said Mr. Satie.

And every day for the rest of the visit, Mr. Satie, Rosalie, and Conrad painted their pictures.

During his lifetime, my good friend Mr. Satie traveled all over the world and had many adventures. I am honored that he chose me to pass them on to you. If some of the people he meets on his journeys look or sound familiar, I'm not the least bit surprised.

T.deP. N.H.